Hazel Hutchins

Dušan Petričić

annick press

toronto + new york + vancouver

For Evan
—H.H.

For my late professor Mileta Sajić
with great appreciation.
—D.P.

Evan had a brand new set of crayons, perfect in every way until...

SNAP!

He tried ordering
the brown crayon
back together.

He tried pressing
the brown crayon
back together.

He tried taping
the brown crayon
together.

Nothing worked.

Finally, he held it out
and stared at it—
hard.

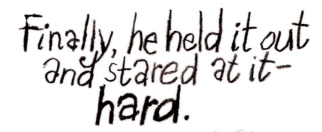

As if by magic,
something changed.

One broken crayon
became two crayons.

A piece was crushed—

SCRITCH!

Evan made furry spots.

And when pieces lost their wrappers, Evan found ways to scootch them sideways across the page.

Sometimes
surprising things
appeared beneath.

Evan now had a mixed-up, messy, one-or-more of every color set of crayons. He kept right on coloring and drawing until...

He tried
fishing it out.

He tried
coaxing it out.

He tried
breaking it out.

Green was gone
for good.

Evan felt like throwing things.
But instead, he scribbled.

Red,
orange,
yellow,
no green,
blue,
purple,
brown,
black.

Red, orange, yellow, no green, blue, pur...
He stopped and stared.
Once again, as if by magic, something had changed.

Where yellow and blue crossed, there was green.

Evan became
so interested in
mixing colors
that he didn't
actually see
the black
crayon
disappear.

And once he knew
that red and yellow
could be used as back-up,
he himself used up
all the orange!

And purple monsters were so perfectly putrid with red and blue mixed in that he just kept working...

...without noticing
an unusual visitor.

WHOOSH—
a sudden gust of wind
came next.
Evan sprawled
across the paper
to protect things.
But the last of brown
and purple were swept away.

Evan now had a very small set of crayons— red, yellow, blue. They were the exact three colors that could still make an entire rainbow.

But when it was finished, the pieces were very, very tiny.

This time
a truly special change
would be needed.
He waited
and watched
and hoped.

And yet,
even while
he hoped,
Evan knew
it wasn't
really
about magic.

He looked at the pieces in every way he could think of – sideways, backwards...

...and, finally, standing on his head. Suddenly, his thoughts flipped upside down.

Which is
when Evan,
all on his own,
turned an ending...

... into a beginning.